The Killer's Identity

L.W

Copyright © 2023 by L.W

ISBN: 979-8-9868798-5-7 (sc)
ISBN: 979-8-9868798-6-4 (eBook)

All rights reserved. No part of this publication may be reproduced, distributed, or transmitted in any form or by any means, including photocopying, recording, or other electronic or mechanical methods, without the prior written permission of the author, except in the case of brief quotations embodied in critical reviews and certain other non-commercial uses permitted by copyright law.

www.writeandreleasepublishing.com

I want to dedicate this book to my role model Jessie Mae
Williams. Wish you were here to celebrate with me. Love you.

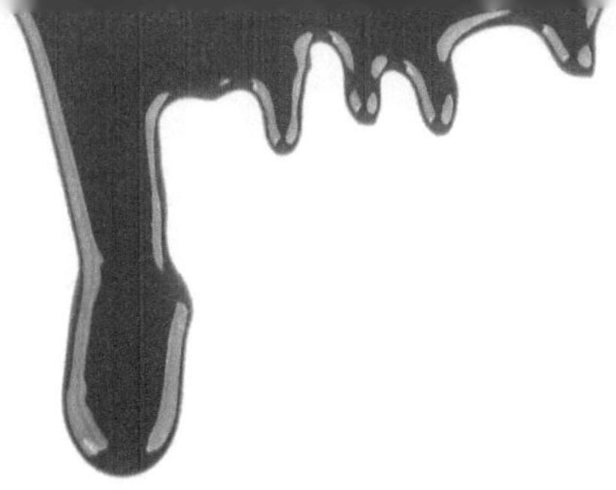

Chapter 1

Tied to a chair, struggling to get free, and with tears running down her cheeks Anne listens for the kidnapper to come back. The sound of footsteps suddenly appears and is getting louder with each step. Her heart starts to pound faster and harder as if it is trying to get away even though the rest of her cannot seem to move. Difficult to know the difference between her heartbeat and the footsteps, as she frantically tries to squeeze her wrists out of the handcuffs. In pitch-black darkness, two hands reach out and grab her by the shoulders, starts to shake and she lets out a loud curling scream. She shuts her eyes tight when he grabbed her but decided she wanted to see the eyes of the man who took her. She opens her eyes, not to a cold lifeless stare of a stranger but to the familiarity of concern and compassion in his eyes. Familiarity because she knew those eyes, they belonged to Mike Cunningham, her partner with the Federal Bureau of Investigation.

Waking up early, only after laying down for five hours before, Mike slaps the alarm clock that is blaring at him from the nightstand next to the bed. Grunting as he sits up, he says his morning prayers adding to it the soon capture of the individual responsible for the series of murders his team has been investigating. Mike Cunningham and Anne Jackson have been tracking the murderer for over a decade. Even though he is loving all the time they are spending together alone on the road, he is sick of these hotel rooms. As he starts to get up, he hears a struggle happening in the next room. He grabs his gun from the drawer of the nightstand and heads to the room that belongs to Anne. He tries the doorknob of their adjoining room, but it is locked from her side, so he kicks it open. He scans the room and sees only Anne and she's having another one of her night terrors.

"Annie! Annie! Wake up. Are you alright? You're having one of those dreams again. I wish you would talk to someone about them," Mike pleads.

Mike standing 6 foot 5 inches and weighing 280 pounds of muscle would scare any woman if she woke up to him shaking her, but not Anne. Mike would never hurt her, she was certain of it. He is in love with her, but he thinks she is unaware of his feelings for her. He has been her partner ever since they graduated from the police academy in Memphis, Tennessee in 2000. While moving his hands off her shoulder she sits up and rubs her face with both hands.

"Yeah, I'm ok. It was only a bad dream not like the others," she tells him. He walks to get her a cup of coffee while still trying to convince her to seek help for her nightmares. Exhausted from a lack of sleep, she looked around a brightly lit room with a very modern look but foreign from the normal semi-lit earthy feel of her apartment back home in Memphis. Being on the road is always hard on her, especially in the mornings after dreaming of the monster she has been chasing for the past decade. The one good thing about being here is she would get to see her twin sister and best friend because they lived here in Georgia. Looking at Mike in the kitchen area brewing her favorite cup of Joe she could not help but wonder if continuing to be partners was the right thing for them both. She cares deeply for him as a friend but is afraid to commit to a relationship with anyone.

"I think that would be a good idea if I had no one to confide in but I do. When it gets too bad, I call my sister and talk to her about it when she is not busy," she says to reassure him.

She has someone who looks exactly like her to whom she can express her deepest darkest fears. Anna Jackson, her twin sister, vowed never to tell anyone about her nightmares so that her job would not be affected.

After getting dressed, Mike knocks on the door he previously kicked in, for permission to enter. Handing her another cup of coffee Mike reminds her they have a meeting with the police chief of Atlanta Georgia to be briefed on the several unsolved murders that seemed to be linked with the others eight bodies found in the six other states going back as far as ten years ago.

"Hey, earth to Anne. Are you sure you got enough rest?" Mike asks as he is handing her the jacket that was laying on the top of the sofa by the door.

"Yeah, I did. I was just daydreaming. I'm ok," Anne says as she takes the jacket from him and heads to the door.

Moving as fast as she could she heard a phone ring and mike answered. The short responses and his tone led her to believe that whoever he was talking to was passing on bad news and not a break in the case. Closing the door behind him he tells her that call was from Captain Santana. "Dispatch just got a call about an abandoned vehicle on the side of the road in Central Park," Mike informs her.

"Okay, does it belong to our victim?" Anne asks. confusingly because they were not there to work in the motor vehicle department.

"No. It belongs to a guy named Fred Simmons 62- years- old approximately 6"2" medium build," Mike says.

"So why are they calling us? There's nobody there?" Anne asks.

Looking at Anne in that matter-of-fact way. "No, but he is ex-military with the same tattoo of the emblem of an anchor with a thick rope intertwined around it," Mike responds.

"Oh no. Not another one," Anne says.

In the precinct, a team rushes to find out everything they can about Fred. They knew if they were dealing with the same suspect, they only had 72 hours before his body would be found. The torture they go through is enough to make a covert operative give up all their secrets. Evidence showed they are bound and tased repeatedly, fingernails are pulled off one by one. They are whipped most likely with a spiked whip, and all of this was done right before the killer cut off their penis and left them to bleed to death. Anne and the rest of the team hoped that something about Fred could help them find him before it was too late.

"Who called in the missing person's report?" Anne asks as they rush into the room where everyone was working frantically to find Fred.

"The wife did after she got a call from his job asking why he wasn't at work," Captain Santana responded. They had officers on phone calls digging into Fred's background. Other officers were on the street searching. The commotion in the room was like something off a TV show. They followed Cpt. Santana through the maze of desks.

"Here are a couple of desks you could use," Captain Santana suggests.

"So far, we haven't been able to find any other connection between Fred and the other victims except for the Navy," Santana continues.

They all served around the same time at the Millington Naval Base, but they could not find any other evidence that linked them together. As far as they could gather the victims did not even know each other. With basically no leads they turned to the navy for help but haven't gotten too much assistance besides what they already know.

"I got guys out at the crash site and surrounding area in hopes that someone saw or knows something," Santana adds.

"We're going to head over to the crash site," Anne says.

On the way to the crash site, Anne wondered since there was no evidence of defensive wounds on the other victims, how could practically healthy ex-navy men be taken so easily. Arriving at the crash site the amount of officers present made Anne feel hopeful. The officer in charge of the search met Anne and Mike.

"How's it going?" Mike asks as he extends his hand for a handshake.

"No luck," the officer answers as he shakes Mike's hand.

"We're going to just have a look at the car," Anne says.

"Sure, right this way," says the officer as he guides them to Fred's car.

The search went on for hours and they couldn't find anything.

"It's been hours and not one clue as to what happened or where he could be. I think we should focus our attention on maybe finding a link between the victims," Mike suggested.

"No, let's span out even further. There's got to be something out there that could lead us to find him. He lives 15 minutes from here. He was supposed to be at work at 7 am. His wife stated he left the house at approximately 5:45 am. So that means this accident had to have happened around 6 am. That means it's been five hours since he went missing," Anne says, staring off into the wooded area across the street from where the car was found.

Chapter 2

THE FIRST MURDER HAPPENED IN Memphis, TN when they were rookie detectives in the homicide division. They were dispatched to a call about a body being found downtown in a parking garage near Beale St. When they arrived, it was a white male mid to late 40s covered in a blue silk sheet with his feet and hands tied together behind his back.

"Have you identified the body yet?" Anne asked Officer Shaw, the first officer who responded to the scene.

Mike surveyed the scene and took notes on what the officer was saying.

"56-year-old Stan Stevens owns his own trucking company according to this business card in his wallet. The medical examiner gives the time of death as 48 hours ago. It looks as if he was beaten and tortured," Officer Shaw stated.

"Who found him?" Anne asked.

"City workers picking up trash early Wednesday morning," Officer Shaw answered.

Looking at the scene there was nothing significant about it. It was the biggest parking lot downtown with no buildings close by, but shuttle stops for pick-ups.

Anne bent down and pulled the sheet back from his face to have a look.

"I thought I've seen it all until now," says Cathy Stevens, Shelby County Medical Examiner.

"There are seven sets of what appears to be a grouping of six puncture wounds, in a rectangular shape, along the abdomen and back areas," Cathy continued.

"The pattern bruising on both wrists and ankles is from being bound together," Cathy said, shaking her head.

"If you look closely, there are several marks two inches apart on his neck and upper chest area most likely from a taser," Cathy ended.

"All of his fingernails were pulled off," Cathy continued while taking in a deep breath.

"Is there something in his mouth?" Anne asked Cathy as she lifted the tape from the side of his mouth.

"Pictures!" Cathy yelled as she gently pulled the tape from his mouth to preserve evidence and gasped.

"What is it?" Anne asked.

Cathy is too stunned to answer right away, it takes her a minute to regain her composure.

"I guess actually seeing a man with his own genitals stuffed in his mouth is not your normal homicide." Cathy finally responded.

"Are you able to give us an approximate time of death?" Mike chimed in trying not puke.

"I would say about two days ago," Cathy answered.

While Cathy had the body transported for autopsy, Mike and Anne stayed behind at the scene. Surveying of the scene took several hours. The crime scene technicians searched the entire parking lot. They collected so much evidence that it would take weeks, maybe months to process. Mike had received a call from Cathy with the results from the autopsy. They hoped that DNA evidence was found that would lead to the killer as he placed the call on speaker.

"Tell me you got good news," Mike said.

"Cause of death is exsanguination. Likely from when his penis was cut off," Cathy answered.

"Meaning he was still alive when they did it," Anne stated in disbelief.

A thorough search of the crime scene gave them no clues to the most important question…who did it.

Chapter 3

ANNE AND ANNA JACKSON ARE 33-year-old African American identical twins raised by their mom, Laura Jackson, and never know who their father was. Growing up in Millington, Tennessee was tough for two girls who didn't have a father to protect, guide, and teach them. There were times they wished they had a father, but none of the guys their mom brought home stuck around. The ones that did stay couldn't wait until they left. The story they got from their mother about their father was enough for any girl to stay away from all men. Anne and Anna were raised in a trailer park not too far from Millington Naval Base. Tasha Williams, their best friend and next-door neighbor, was their only friend. The three girls became very close. Tasha's mother, Katrina Williams, knew what was happening in their home, but she never questioned them. Katrina noticed the girls would eat more than a normal little girl would when they came over to play. That is when she started paying attention to what was happening next door. She tried to help the twins out as much as she could.

She would make sure the girls ate, showered for school, and back in their room so Laura wouldn't notice before she got up and took her anger out on them. Their mother Laura was a waitress and an alcoholic. She drank daily even while pregnant with the twins. After giving birth she never quite took on the motherly role. She provided the necessary things they needed but nothing more. As Anne and Anna grew up Anne took on the motherly role in taking care of Anna. In school they both got good grades and participated in extracurricular activities that did not cost to join.

"Mom, we have a home game today. Are you going to be there?" Anna would ask.

"Oh no, sweetie I'm sorry I have to work a double shift tonight," Laura said as she searched the kitchen for a bottle of whiskey not even looking at Anna. I only need a couple of sips before work, she thinks, and I will be fine until I get off tonight.

"Mom, what are you looking for?" Anna asked.

"Nothing!" Laura shouted. "You girls hurry up and get ready for school before you're late,"

She never liked going anywhere where she could not take her bottle. When the girls were in middle school, they starred in "A Night Before Christmas".

"Woo hoo!" Laura shouted. "Look at my girls, aren't they adorable or what!"

Anne was so embarrassed that she ran off stage crying. Anna on the other hand stood on stage with tears welling in her eyes and stared out at the crowd with anger. Security showed up to get her to leave but Laura kicked and screamed as they dragged her out.

"I have every right to be here just like the rest of the parents! I am the mother of the twins up there. They are my girls, and I can see them perform if I want!" She shouted while trying to fight off security.

Demands to be let go is all the girls could hear from backstage. Laura yanked her arm from one of the guards and started to stagger away digging through her purse for her keys. She started drinking more when the girls started asking about who their father was. She put it off at first and told them that she would tell them when they got older. The guilt made her drink more because she could not bear the truth. What the twins would think of her if they knew the truth. When the girls were 12-years-old they did not let her off the hook. She nervously tried to get out of telling them her version of her past. So, she told them to sit down and what she was about to tell them would be hard to hear. Maybe a little scary, but she felt it was time they heard the truth about their father.

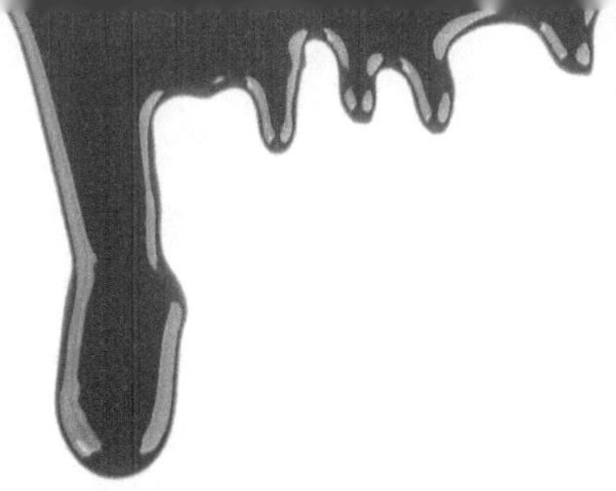

Chapter 4

"LATER, GIRLS," A 19-YEAR-OLD LAURA said to her best friends as they leave the college campus library. She decided to walk by herself that night because the library was not too far from her dorm. No attacks had been reported so every student felt safe to walk alone at night. She walked down the corridor to the Harmony Building which housed over 150 students where her room was at the very end of the hall. As she got closer, she noticed the exit door was cracked ajar. It did not have anything to do with her, so she ignored it and went into her room. As she started to relax, she thought if security caught the door open, she would be blamed because it was right next to her room. She threw her books down on the bed, turned around, and headed back to the exit door to close it. She reached out to close the door, but it would not move. She looked down and noticed that there was a brick at the bottom keeping the door ajar. She looked out to see if someone was standing out close by the door, but no one was there. She bent down to move the brick out of the way when she heard rustling in the bushes. Before she could straighten up to see what the noise was, she felt a sharp pain in the back of her head and then total darkness.

Laura started to moan and mumble something that no one can understand. She tried to reach up and grab the back of her head, but her arm was restricted. She looked down and saw her hand was cuffed to a chair. She tried to move the other arm and it was cuffed just like the other. She started to come to and realized that not only were her hands cuffed, but her mouth was duct-taped, and her legs were bound together. She looked around frantically trying to figure out where she was, but it was too dark and the only sound she heard was her panicked breathing. She heard footsteps approaching and she could not quite tell which way they were coming from.

Suddenly a small light shined in front of her, and it got bigger the closer it got. A man 6"2" wearing a crisp white Navy sailor's uniform holding a bag in his hand appeared from behind that light. When she first saw him, she thought she was saved, and her eyes told him the same thing. He moved with precision all while he stared at her. He took a set of coveralls out of the bag and put on this suit which looks like he was going into a biohazard zone. The coveralls are covered in dark spots which look like blood splatter. He comes up to Laura and just stares at her. She started wiggling and gesturing her head towards her hands as to say get me out of these.

"I will let you go," He said.

She breathed a sense of relief.

"But not until I'm done with you," He informed her right before he punched her in the jaw.

She tried to scream in pain not understanding why this was happening to her. He let her hands out of the chains and untied her from the chair. He grabbed her by her hair and yanked her out of the chair and threw her to the ground. That's when the torture began. Laura had rehearsed this story to tell the twins so many times she almost started to believe it really happened.

Chapter 5

Fred Simmons, a 62-year-old postal worker of 24 years, gets up for work around 4 am just like any other day. He sneaks out of bed very softly to not wake Daisy, his wife of 30 years. He heads to the bathroom to shower while singing his favorite song "Tutti Frutti" by Little Richard. He steps out of the shower, brushes his teeth and combs over the bald spot he's been desperately trying to hide with no success. Today the balding spot doesn't bother him as much as it usually does because today is his birthday and his last day working. Every year his family throws the most awesome parties for him, and each year outdoes the year before. He knows that his gift is going to be something spectacular. He doesn't know exactly what it is, but he can just feel it. Usually, Fred will give Daisy a peck on the cheek before he heads out the door. Today she rolls over to his surprise and kisses him as if he will be gone for a long time.

"Wow! I would have said I was retiring every day if I knew I would get this type of greeting in the morning," Fred says as he strokes her cheek, and he stares into her eyes.

"Hurry home dear," Daisy whispers.

"I will," Fred replies.

Fred takes the same route to work which goes past Central Park overlooking the riverside under the lights on the running path feeling on top of the world. He looks out onto the water just for a second cause no one else is on the road this time of morning anyway. As he turns his eyes back on the road, he slams the brakes to the floor of the car. It screeches and starts to spin out of control as he tries to get a handle on the car. It comes to a halt on the opposite side of the road in the bushes. Smoke was coming from the engine of his light gray 1935 Chevy Corvette he got for his birthday last year. Fred takes a second to catch his breath. He gets out of the car to assess the damages and remembers what made him swerve in the first place. Someone was standing in the middle of the road. He rushes back over to see if the person was hurt. "God please don't let me hit them!" He says out loud without realizing it. Amazingly they were still standing in the same spot on the road.

"Hey, are you alright?" Fred yells as he gets closer.

The person says nothing just stands there with their head down motionless. The closer he got, he started to move a little slower because he is getting an eerie feeling about this whole situation. A part of him screams "run get back into your car and get the hell out of here!" The other half says "this person may need help and if you don't help something bad could happen.

You don't want that on your conscience," As he reaches a hand up to tap the person, he feels a slight sting on the side of his neck.

"What in the world?" Fred says as everything starts to spin and go dark. He falls to the ground unconscious.

Chapter 6

STACY AND DREW WILSON, A newlywed couple that loved to hike so that is what they did for their honeymoon, in Central Park. Even though they knew that it was prohibited to do so, they figured they would not get caught so headed there around 3 am to set up camp. They took a cab, so their car is not inconspicuously parked. They were going to be there for a couple of days, and they did not want their car to be towed or someone thinking they needed rescuing. The only people that knew where they were was their parents just in case something did happen, and they did not come back. About a mile up into the woods, past the river, they see a huge plastic container with a dolly next to it. They look around to see if they notice anyone else there who may have come to camp or already camped out there and may need help. Drew was about to yell out "hello," but Stacy grabbed his forearm.

"No, don't do that. Let's just get out of here and go about our business," She whispers as if someone was listening.

"What if someone needs help and calls out to us because they cannot move?" He looks at her baffled. Stacy was always the one going out of her way to help everyone even the smallest of insects she cared for.

"No, who camps with a plastic container and a dolly? That does not make any sense. It just seems weird to me. I can't explain it but let's just go," She demanded.

"You watch too much forensic files. It has you all jumpy," Drew told her as he shook his head dismissively.

They quickly move on hoping that no one hears their footsteps while cracking sticks with each step as they climb up the steep path. Focused on the items they quickly headed to their campsite.

"I can't find my wallet!" Drew said as he searched all his pockets. "It must have fallen out on the way up here. Stay here, I'll go back and get it," He said.

"You are not leaving me by myself! Are you crazy?!" she says as she gets up to leave with him.

"It will only take me a few minutes, Stace. There aren't anybody burying psychos out here. You'll be fine," Drew tries to reassure her.

To be honest, he had a funny feeling about them being out there, but he didn't want her to freak out more than she already was.

As they near the area where he dropped his wallet, they see someone about to leave with the cooler and dolly.

"See, it's just a lady. She probably camped out here too and had a lot of stuff and needed the dolly to move the huge plastic container," Drew said quietly after spitting out his gum. He still thought something was off about what they were seeing.

"No, something just does not seem right. Let her leave. Hopefully she didn't notice your wallet and we can grab it afterward," Stacy says.

The wallet was still there so they grabbed it and left and did not speak again about what happened.

Chapter 7

Anne wondered if they would find Fred in time. Finding nothing concrete in Fred's car Anne and Mike head back to the scene of the accident. As Mike talked to an officer with the search party, Anne stared out into the woods on the other side of the road. She thought maybe they had been looking on the wrong side of the park. She took off across the road, pulled out her flashlight and started to search. Mike went back to let Anne know there was no progress, but she was not there. He turned and asked a couple of officers if they saw where she went. They shake their heads no. He looked off across the street to the other side of the park. He started across Johnson Road away from Proctors Creek. He took out his flashlight and his phone to check for her location, which showed she was heading left and yelled her name. The location feature on the phones were a lifesaver, especially for law enforcement looking for their partners who may not be able to respond with their location.

Anne thought she heard someone calling her name. She stopped and looked back but saw nothing but trees. At that moment she realized she took off into the woods in a park that she was just as familiar with as she is with her biological father. She turned back to the path she was headed in. It sounded like it was about to start raining and she knew if there was any evidence out there it would have been washed away. As she continued to walk, she looked down and saw a tire tread in the dirt right off the running path. She bent down to examine it. She noticed a chewed-up piece of gum to the left of the tire tread. Not sure why, but she felt it was important, so she bagged it as evidence. She looked back at the print and noticed it was too small to be from a motorcycle but wider than a bicycle. Why would someone be wheeling something like that through these woods she thought. In the next instant, huge drops of rain started to fall. "No, no, no, no, no!" Anne said as she pulled out her phone and snapped a picture before the water washed away the features. A hand grabbed her shoulder. She jumped and whirled around aiming her gun in that direction.

"Whoa," Mike said, holding his hands in the air. "I've been calling your name from way back there. It was like you were in a trance or something. Didn't you hear me?"

"No," Anne replied.

"Why did you take off like that? Did you see something?" Mike asked looking around to survey the area.

"No, I just had a hunch," Anne said.

"Well let's get out of here before they have to start a search party just to find us," Mike said.

Leaving the woods in a hurry, Anne felt they were closer to finding Fred at that moment, and leaving the scene would be a big mistake.

Chapter 8

Drew Smith was home getting ready for work when he saw the news broadcast about the missing man, Fred Simmons. The newscaster was showing a video of live footage of the scene of the wreck. He dropped his coffee cup, which shatters on the floor as he spits it out. "It can't be?" He whispered to himself standing there in disbelief.

Stacy came out of the bedroom to see what was wrong. "Are you ok? What's wrong?"

She asks with a confused look on her face. He points to the television. He suddenly becomes frantic that not only is the campsite on the news but there was a possible kidnapping in the area. It terrifies him that they could be the only people who have seen the identity of the kidnapper. "No one knows we were there, not even the kidnapper if there was one," she reassures him. "Maybe the man was in shock from the accident and went and got treatment and he could be listed as John Doe from possible amnesia," she says. After convincing Drew that their identities would never be disclosed to anyone, they both went about their day and didn't give it another thought.

A couple of days went by and even though Stacy was convinced that she was right Drew wasn't totally on board. They were both perfectionists and didn't like to be taken by surprise. It was dinner time, and the newly married couple was putting away the dishes after eating. Stacy decided to check her email while Drew showered. When Drew stepped out of the shower, Stacy began to talk about the next day's tasks that needed to be completed when there was a knock at the door.

"I'll get it," Stacy says while heading to the door.

She was confused about who it could be because they weren't expecting company. As Stacy opens the door, she is already saying the usual line "I'm sorry that person..." She gets out the first few words when she looks up and sees the lady that was wheeling the cooler in the woods at the door. Drew hears the sound of something shattering on the floor from the bedroom.

"Honey, are you ok?" He says and gets no answer.

It was like Stacy had vanished in thin air because there is no sound of life, only the TV playing the news.

"Hon!" he shouts. "What's going on? Is everything okay?" he continues to ask as he makes his way to the front. He comes around the corner from the long hallway that only takes a minute until you reach the living room. He reaches the end and turns towards the right which leads to the front door. There is broken glass everywhere around where Stacy was standing frozen almost as if she's been turned into stone. He wasn't sure if she was aware of where she was, but he noticed the forefinger on her right hand was twitching like crazy. That only happens when she's scared or very nervous about something.

"Hon, who is it?" words that broke her statute-like state. She turned to Drew "Oh yeah, I'm okay just clumsy. I dropped the plate as I was opening the door,"

She turns back to the unexpected guests on the other side of the door. Drew stepped into the clearing to see who it was, he couldn't believe his eyes. It was like all the air in his lungs was just knocked right out of him. He found it almost impossible to take the next breath.

Chapter 9

THE SOUND OF POLICE CARS flying by rang out even in the 3-story abandoned building. Starting to come too, Fred did not know what to think. Trying to figure out what happened and where he was, he focused on what he could hear. He knew that he was tied to a chair with his mouth and eyes covered. He heard footsteps approaching so he kept his slumped as if he was still unconscious. Suddenly the tape that was wrapped around his eyes had been ripped off.

"Wake up!" a lady's voice yelled at him. "I want you fully aware of what's about to happen to you," she said.

He focused his eyes on the light and ignored the pain from what he could see was duct tape that had been ripped from his face. He wanted to say something to her, but only mumbled sounds came out. He still had duct tape around his mouth. She cut a slit in the tape between his lips. "I will give you whatever you want," he said. He was not sure if that is what she heard. Whatever she injected him with was strong because he can barely keep his head up let alone speak clearly. If I can just explain to her, she got the wrong guy he thought. He kept trying to explain but his words were slurred. She did not say anything else, just stood and stared at him. His head still bobbing he felt the wind get knocked out of him. Coughing up blood he tried to say wait and he got hit again. Why me? That was the last thought that crossed his mind when he felt the worst pain imaginable between his legs. Fred screamed as if nothing was partially wrapped around his mouth. He looked down to see that his penis was gone and passed out.

Chapter 10

UNHAPPY ABOUT THEIR HOME LIFE and upbringing, the twins worked hard towards a better life for themselves. Anna Jackson chose to be an Ultimate Fighting Championship (UFC) fighter.

She was always supportive of her sister's career path but was more concerned with being able to protect herself. Afraid that what happened to their mom could happen to her, she solely focused on self-defense. Unaware of all the attention she was getting while training, people were taking notes and sharing her name and videos on social media. One day her trainer approached her about fighting professionally, she was against it at first, but when he explained to her how she could train and get paid for it. She was all in.

Anna Jackson sitting in the locker room, staring off into space instead of getting prepared for her match. People seem to be buzzing around her as if she was not there to give input on some aspect of her fight. Not paying attention to anyone, her mind drifted back to her childhood. As her trainer greases her face it reminded her of the moment she started to fight back when she was younger. When she was in middle school there was a bully named George who would always pick on her. One day during recess she was standing off to herself when she gets pushed down from behind. She tried to break her fall with her hands, but she hit her face against a rock. Wincing from the pain in her hands and her head, she gets up and dusts herself off. She turned to see who pushed her and she saw George and three of his friends standing there laughing. Usually, when they picked on her she would cry and tell her sister. Not that day. She was not sure why she felt different, but she did. She was angry instead of scared. Tears welled up in her eyes and she bawled up her fists and punched George in the face. George yells out in pain while his friends stood and watched as Anna beat him up. She did not stop punching him until a teacher aide came to pull her off of him. At home, sitting in the bathroom, Anne cleans up the cut on Anna's head while telling her she was proud of her. Anna could not. They tried everything they knew how to get their mother to love them, but nothing worked. Anna blamed the neglect she felt from her mother as a kid on her mother's rapist, her father. She always thought about what she would do if she ever got her hands on the man who brutally beat and raped her mother. This thought she had before every fight, and she took that rage out on her opponents.

Chapter 11

It was a long shot, but Anne submitted the chewed-up gum she found in the park before it started raining into evidence. Linda, one of the crime techs owed her a favor so she told her to call the moment she gets a match. Not sure why she even picked it up, but her gut was telling her that it was something important about that spit-out piece of gum. So, when Linda from the crime lab called her cell phone with the results of the DNA, she gave her the name of Drew Smith. Something inside of her was excited but not sure why so she just kept it to herself until she knew for sure. If it turned out to be nothing, no harm no foul but if it did, she would tell Mike about how they came to the lead. A background check on Drew Smith produced only his prior military service. He spent 4 years in the US Navy. Arriving at the home of Drew and Stacy Smith, Anne rang the doorbell and waited for a response. Someone had to be home because there were sounds from the TV and someone washing dishes came through the door. Mike was about to ask a question when the door opened. A lady already saying "I'm sorry" appears but the moment she laid eyes on Anne she dropped a plate and stared at her like she'd seen a ghost. As they waited to hear what else she was going to say, a man's voice came from behind her. He was asking if she was okay, but she just stood there with no movement whatsoever.

Anne and Mike look at each other in confusion and when they turn back to look at the lady Anne decides to break the awkward silence.

"Hi, I'm Agent Anne Jackson and this is my partner Agent Mike Cunningham with the FBI. Are you Stacy Smith?" she asks.

Anne noticed no response, no movement from Stacy. Just as she was about to ask again, a man came around the corner and stepped into the clearing. When he gets to the door, he says 'Hon are you ok?" When he looks and sees them standing there, he becomes a statue just like the lady. Stacy snaps out of it "Oh yes, I'm sorry. I thought you were someone else. Please forgive me for staring," She said awkwardly.

Anne figured it had to be that they had mistaken her for her sister Anna. She's famous and people love her but most of her fans either don't know or forget she has an identical twin sister. "Are you Stacy and Drew Smith?" Anne asks again since they didn't get an answer earlier.

"Yes," Drew says shakily.

"Could we come in for a minute? We just have a couple of questions to ask you," Mike chimes in now interested in hearing what they had to say. The last time they went to question total strangers it led them to capture a heinous murderer who had eluded authorities for months and all because Anne found some insignificant piece of evidence. The agents step into the living room and stand patiently while the couple picks up the pieces of glass and whispers hysterically to each other. It was almost to the point that Anne and Mike thought the Smiths forgot two federal agents were in their home watching them. Mike and Anne give each other the look that they know something and turn back to the Smiths.

"What can we do for you?" Drew asks as Stacy eagerly awaits a response to his question. "We are investigating a missing person's report," Anne says as she hands him a picture of Fred. "We are wondering if you know or have ever seen him before,"

Stacy grabs the picture from Drew, without even looking at it and shakes her head no. Drew, who Anne noticed did not look at the picture, also shakes his head as Stacy gives the picture back to her.

"Well can I ask where the two of you were two nights ago?" Anne asks now, sure they were on the right track. Drew gets this terrified look on his face and looks at Stacy worriedly.

"Ugh, we were together celebrating a late honeymoon. We... we just got married recently," Drew studders.

"Where did you go?" Mike asks.

Stacy gives Drew this look like he better say the right thing but once he spoke her mouth gaped open in disbelief.

"We were in Central Park," Drew confesses like he just admitted to committing a crime.

"What were you doing in the park that day?" Anne asks.

"We camped there because we couldn't afford to go anywhere. We knew it was illegal, but we love the outdoors, and it was the only weekend we both had off so we decided to make the best of it you know..." Drew blabbers on and on.

"Sir, sir, we just wanted to know if you guys had seen anything that was suspicious while you were out there. It doesn't matter if you think it's insignificant. Please, anything you know may help find this man," Anne says, trying to put Drew at ease.

Once again there was that look on their faces as if what Anne just said turned them both into stone. Federal agent! Drew thinks to himself. It can't be and now she's asking if we saw anything. You! He wanted to yell but he couldn't bring himself to say anything. He notices Stacy is speechless also.

"No, no, nothing," Drew and Stacy say at the same time.

"Well, how long were you guys out there? Maybe you heard something," Mike asks.

"Just one day!" Drew lied.

Anne notices that Stacy looks at Drew awkwardly, but she agrees with him.

"Yeah, we just went for one day just to get away," Stacy says, cutting her eyes from Drew to Anne.

"Yea, we didn't hear anything except for the normal woodsy noise of crickets, cicadas, and an occasional owl or two," Drew says.

After a couple more questions the agents decided to end the visit.

"Just think on it some more and if either of you remembers anything, please call," Mike says as he hands Drew his business card. Anne was sure they were holding something back and she was determined to find out what it was.

Once Mike and Anne left the couple was silent for what seems like forever not knowing what to say about what just happened.

"I don't think she believes us," Drew says nervously.

Going back and forth on what they should do they were at odds and scared out of their minds.

"Do you think she saw us out there?" Stacy says frantically.

"No, I don't think so. We were in the trees far back from the clearing and there's no possible way to see through that," Drew says trying to convince himself.

"Let's just see if they are who they say they are," He says trying to reassure her.

So, they get onto the computer and research agents Anne Jackson and Mike Cunningham. They google Anne Jackson, and what they found they couldn't believe it.

"Two of them!" Stacy whispers almost to herself.

"What if the one we saw was not the agent, but her sister?" Drew asks not taking his eyes off the screen.

There it was articles, videos, interviews, and pictures of both but mostly Anna, her twin the famous UFC fighter. They read everything there was on her and watched every video and interview they could find. But how could Drew be sure? How could he tell the agent that he saw the possible kidnapper and oh by the way it's your twin sister. Torn over what to do, Drew, who is a veteran, consistently expresses the need to come clean to the agents. Stacy feels that they should stay out of it.

"She can't prove what we did and did not see!" Stacy says matter-of-factly.

"How do you think they found us?" Drew says, hoping to convince Stacy to see things his way.

"We cleaned up everything. We left nothing behind that could lead to us," Drew says

On the way back to the car Mike and Anne discuss everything that just happened.

"Did you see how they looked at us?' Mike smirks.

"I know, like they saw a ghost or something," Anne was still confused over the entire interaction.

"They didn't respond normally like you would answer your door. They were scared for some reason," Anne says.

"They know something," Mike responded as he opened the car door to get in.

"Yeah, and we're going to find out what it is," she tells him.

Anne didn't want to point out the fact that Stacy stared at her most of the time while they were in their home. Even though she gets that a lot from her sister's fans, something about this interaction seemed off. Usually, seconds after the shock of seeing their favorite celebrity they would get excited. They would jump up and down, scream, yell, cry and rush in for a hug and ask for autographs and pictures all before she can say "I'm not Anna but her twin Anne and I'm a cop,"

They do more research on the couple and investigate their entire lives. Their family, friends, employers, coworkers, and anyone and anything attached to them.

"Let's call it a night. It's getting late," Mike yawns as he gets up from his desk.

"Yeah, we can pick up from here in the morning," Anne agrees.

Chapter 12

THE NEXT MORNING, MIKE AND Anne meet back at the office and get started with looking into Drew and Stacy Smith.

"I think we should bring them into interrogation," Mike says. "Give them the sense that this is serious, and we know they are hiding something and need to know what it is," He continues getting frustrated with coming up empty at every turn.

"There is nothing here that suggests they would be tied up in anything criminal. I can't even find a parking ticket. You saw how the husband blurted out what they did, and you can tell the wife wasn't too happy about it," Anne says, analyzing every detail of their encounter with the Smiths.

"We should go at him because he's the one with the conscience that will eat him up if he lies about something," Mike says.

"Well, we need to question him soon because time is of the essence," Anne says as she looks at her watch.

As they were about to go back to the Smiths' residence, Drew is escorted into the squad room by an officer who stated he was here to see them.

Stunned to see Drew, Mike tells the officer to take Drew to one of the interrogation rooms. They look at each other with utter disbelief. They couldn't believe it. It was like the heavens were listening to them or just really wanted them to find Fred and possibly catch a crazed killer. They head to the room where Drew was waiting nervously. Drew is looking around as Mike motions for him to sit in the chair on the other side of the table. Anne sits in the last remaining chair while Mike stands next to Anne. Mike turns around to the 2-way mirror and nods to the officer behind it to make sure the video camera was on and recording.

"Hey, how are you, Mr. Smith? We were just about to pay you another visit when you showed up." Anne says.

"Why?" Drew asks nervously.

Drew just looks between Mike and Anne.

"Well, we were on our way to see you and your wife again. Just to see if either of you remembered anything after we left last night," Anne responded.

They noticed a bit of hesitation and didn't want to scare him into silence.

"We haven't been able to locate Fred Simmons, the man from the accident right where you guys were camping in the woods, nor any evidence that could lead to his whereabouts," Mike adds to try and plead to his consciousness.

Drew looks nervously between the both of them again. Anne can tell it was something Drew wanted to say but was either too afraid to say it or didn't know how to say it. Maybe he knew the individual or individuals that are involved. The possibilities of what he may know are endless. After being in the profession for over 10 years they can tell when someone is hiding something. There were plenty of cases that shook them to their core so they were very confident that what he had to say would not surprise them in any way. Hoping to put Drew at ease, Anne figured they should let him lead the conversation.

"So, what is it that brought you up here to see us? Why don't we start there?" She says.

"Well, we did see something in the woods that night," Drew whispered so low that no one could hear and looked down now afraid to make eye contact.

"You guys said that guy had an accident?" He said a little louder while trying to gain his confidence back.

They didn't say anything, just stared at him calmingly. They could sense his nervousness, but they did not want to pressure him.

Mike was getting more and more impatient, but he knew not to do anything to blow this opportunity.

"Look. I know this may be difficult for you. If you're afraid, we could help you. Just tell us what you saw, and no one will have to know the information came from you if you're worried about someone coming after you and your wife," Anne says to save Mike from bursting at the seams.

It seemed as if every time they said anything Drew just looked back and forth from her to Mike getting more anxious as every second passed.

"Just tell us and we will protect you, I promise," Mike says.

"Is it someone you know or recognized?" Anne chimes in

"Yes. I mean no…ugh…not really," Drew whispers.

"I don't understand. Just start from the beginning and tell us exactly what you saw," Anne says while eagerly leaning forward on the table.

Nervously Drew starts to tell his story. He began with when he and Stacy got married. They both went back to work immediately due to demanding jobs and not enough income or savings to take time off and still be able to pay all their bills. He dives into their life together as if it was suddenly over with. When he gets to how they were having fun and when they heard a noise and saw the individual with the dolly and a large plastic container, Anne's body language changed. Her attention peaked at that point. It was like she was at the movies and the plot has just gotten good and is eager to see what happens next. He continues speaking about how they thought it was odd but for some reason, they were scared and didn't know why. He tells them the lady didn't look dangerous or mad or anything, but they were still afraid to move or make a noise to alert her of their presence.

"Her?" Anne and Mike both repeat to Drew shocked.

When Anne heard the word *her* it was like being punched in the gut. The victims were not small at all and the possibility that a woman was kidnapping, torturing, and killing them was surprising. Despite the heinous nature of the crimes, she was kind of in awe of this mysterious woman and if she had an accomplice.

"You said that you kind of recognized the woman," Mike said, hoping to get the weird gaze Drew had on Anne onto him.

He just continues to look at her now with all seriousness and fear at the same time. Mike looks at her wondering what was going on.

"Who was it Drew?" Mike asks now, convinced that he knew exactly who was in that park that night.

Drew is still looking at Anne "You," he says while wincing now not knowing what was going to happen afterward.

Chapter 13

THE CASE HAS BEEN HEADLINING for months now. Every law enforcement agency wanted in on it and was also keeping tabs on the progress made. It seemed as if they were in that room with Drew for days. Time is a funny thing; it never moves the way you want it to. It had only been 45 minutes from the time Drew walked through the squadron doors to the moment he said that infamous word. "You"

They looked at each other like Drew had suddenly forgotten how to speak English and the language he suddenly switched to has never been heard of.

"Who?" Anne asks hoping that she didn't hear what she thought she just heard.

"You" he said again in a whisper now terrified.

Anne stared at Drew while Mike was staring at Anne confusingly.

"Who?" Mike adds.

"You! Her!" Drew finally spoke up in a tone that everyone was able to hear clearly.

"You. We saw you in the woods with a dolly carrying a plastic container. We waited until we were convinced you were out of sight and then got the hell outta there! We thought we were in the clear and told ourselves that we were just going to stay out of it because we didn't know exactly what we were seeing. When we got home, we saw the news and Stacy decided that it would be best to just not say anything you know. And then you show up at our door asking questions about that night. We just couldn't believe it. We were sure you came to silence us or something. My wife and I panicked after you guys left our house, and we were going to pack up and leave town. I started thinking that maybe that would make things worse for us, plus I don't want to live a life on the run,"

Realizing what he just said, he had to clear it up.

"Not that you're a serial killer. I don't think because after you guys left, we googled you and your partner here and saw that you have an identical twin. So, I figured that I would toss the coin and come in hoping that it wasn't you in the woods but your sister,"

He sighs as if a huge weight had been lifted off his shoulders and he hasn't taken a breath the entire time he was talking. Then he thought *I just accused her sister of kidnapping.*

"Well, not that your sister is a serial killer. It was probably a good reason for her being there that time of night you know. Look at us we were there," He chuckled and ended the story and looked down at his lap sensing he had said enough.

Standing on the other side of the 2-way mirror, a couple of detectives had been joined by Captain Santana. The awkward silence in the interrogation room was deafening. Mike had pulled Anne out of the chair, while telling Drew to hold tight all while Anne was in a trance-like state almost. Anne was still trying to wrap her head around the fact that he said it was her that they'd seen in the woods that night. She tried to figure out what they're angle was. Did they do it and were trying to play witness/victim because they've been found out, to stall or steer the investigation away from them she thought. Consumed by her own thoughts that she didn't notice the bickering back and forth that was going on right next to her.

"Anne!" Captain Fletcher said, trying to snap her back to reality.

Anne looked around, finally noticing the small group that had gathered.

"If anyone understands what I'm about to ask, it should be you. Could there be any truth to what he's saying?" Captain Fletcher asks her.

"Captain!" Mike says with disgust.

"You shouldn't be so quick to accuse someone. Especially a fellow officer. She didn't have anything to do with this! Hell, she's been chasing this son of a bitch for 10 years!" He says now angry. "I want you two in my office now!" Captain Santana ordered.

Judging by the looks in the room she figured Mike was the only one that was sure she was not guilty in any way. Everyone else was coming up with their conclusions about how she could be the serial killer or involved in some way. After having another officer take Drew Smith's statement and letting him go, Anne and Mike wait to hear what is going to happen next. Captain Santana comes into his office and closes the door. Before he could say one word Mike started defending Anne.

"Before he identified Anne, we agreed that he was telling the truth about the fact that he saw something, we just didn't exactly know what it was," Mike tried desperately to take the heat off Anne.

"I'm sorry Mike, I know what you're trying to do but we all know what has to happen," Captain says, cutting him off.

Chapter 14

Susan, a young mother taking her daughter, Sarah to the park for a play date, decided to go through the walking path in Central Park. The path to the playground is covered with tall thick beautiful elm trees as tall as the Heavens. She loves nature and all of its wildlife. Just at that moment, a rat ran across the walk from one side to the other. It scared her so bad that she nearly yanks her daughter's arm out of the socket pulling her away from where the rat ran into the bushes.

"Ooohh, mom what was that!" Sarah asks very excited and curiously as she snatched away from Susan to follow the rodent. Sarah moved so fast that she was already out of arm's reach when Susan tries to grab her again. "Sarah!" Susan yells as she darts off after the little girl to keep her from getting hurt. Oh, what if there's poison ivy or poison oak in these bushes that are going to be a hassle to deal with if she catches it, she's thinking as she carefully makes her way through the bushes to get to Sarah.

"Sarah, come back here! It's not funny anymore," Susan yells.

She realizes that Sarah didn't answer. No sounds were coming from up ahead of her. Panic was starting to set in. Susan was trying hard to fight back the urge to panic as she made her way through the bushes. That once careful moment in the bushes has now turned into a frantic jog. Her eyes jotted left to right as she called out Sarah's name and got no response. Susan was about to give in to a full-on panic and start screaming, the way you would hear when a mother has lost her child. At that moment she saw Sarah standing in a small clearing motionless, like she had been turned into a zombie. Susan notices nothing except Sarah. Susan runs up to her, picks her up and hugs her so tight. She was sure Sarah was going to start squirming and moaning "too tight mom" as she always does.

"Oh, honey you scared mommy. Don't ever do that again. Ok?" Susan says as she strokes her daughter's hair and looks at her overseeing if she has been hurt in any way.

"Ok?" Susan repeats waiting for the *ok mommy* response but getting nothing. She puts her down and looks at her so she can see her face and she just stares straight ahead.

"Sarah, what's wrong? Honey, say something?" Susan pleads in a panic. She turned her head so she could see what Sarah could be looking at. She looked back over her shoulder and what she saw made her fall to the ground. As she started getting up, she grabbed for Sarah to get back as if it was going to come after them. She fumbles for her cell phone to call 911 to tell them that she and her daughter have just found a dead body.

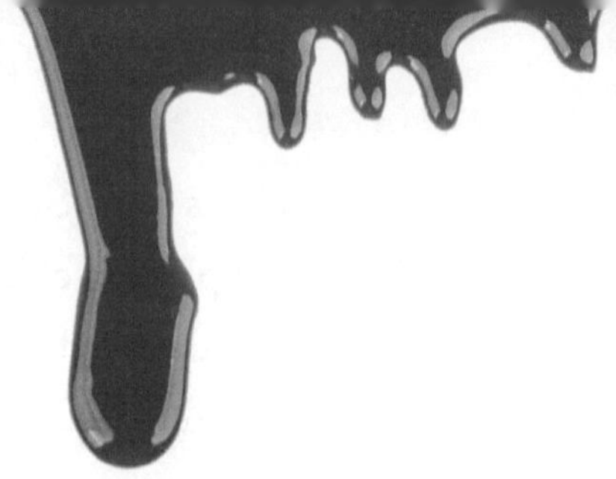

Chapter 15

After that interview with Drew Smith, Anne just couldn't stop thinking about how this could be. There's no way they saw me out there! He must be covering up for himself or someone else! She thought trying to figure out how all of this came to be.

"You know I have to pull you off the case," Captain Fletcher says, pulling her out of her train of thought.

"Uh yeah…wait WHAT!? No, you can't do that to me! I promise you I have nothing to do with this. I've been chasing this monster for almost 10 years!" she pleads.

"I know you have a history with this case. You know every detail like the back of your hand. But this is a turn in the case none of us expected. I understand that you want to bring it to a close but for GOD's sake how are you to remain objective. You've been accused by the only lead we have had in this case. Ok, look I don't believe it was you but until we get to the bottom of it, you're out. I'm sorry," Captain Santana says, trying to make his plea for understanding.

Mike and Anne had worked with the captain on cases in the past and became good friends over time. She knows that the captain will have to report this up the chain of command and she will immediately be taken off the case and brought in for questioning.

"Please don't make me feel bad about what I must do. Plus, you would be biased anyway, and you know it. You know once you're questioned, they will bring your sister in. There is no way you would be allowed to question her," He says matter-of-factly.

The speech he was giving her about why she will be sidelined started to bring tears to her eyes. It's the protocol that when any officer is dealing with a case that involves a family member or friend, they are taken off the case. It all started to feel like one of the nightmares she has. The monster is there somewhere in the shadows lurking waiting to catch her off guard. It wasn't registering that she could be the main suspect and her life would be turned upside down. At that moment it dawned on her that if she could be made a suspect so could her sister.

"OMG Anna," she says to herself as she bolts out of the captain's office. No longer did she care about being off the investigation or possibly being put under arrest, she only cared about getting to her sister before anyone else did. Her sister is her best friend and maybe the captain was right about her not being able to be objective. She knows she didn't do anything and of course, her sister would never, but the justice system works against Black people. She did not want a tactical unit sent out to arrest Anna and somehow, she ended up beaten or worse, dead.

And she did not want to come to the realization her sister could be a serial killer.

Come on Anna pick up pick up! Anne thought while holding her cell phone to her ear.

"Hey what's up, sis?" Anna says a little out of breath picking up her phone that had been ringing off the hook.

"What's wrong?" Anne asked nervously. No way they got to her this quick she thought.

"Nothing's wrong, I just got done training for my next fight. Is everything all right? You've called my phone back-to-back?" Anna asks now worried.

"I need you to meet me in the police station right now. I know you're training but this can't wait," Anne tells her.

"Right now!" Anna responds thinking why can't she just tell me over the phone. It sounded urgent and Anne has never interrupted her especially while training, so she decided to go.

"Ok. Ok, I'm coming," She reassures Anne before hanging up wondering what could be so urgent that she wanted her to come to the station.

Chapter 16

Captain Santana did not want the District Attorney coming down on his head about how this case was mishandled, so he took over until other FBI agents came to replace Anne and Mike.

"I need everything you've got since you've been here on this case," he said to Mike as he ignored the sound of the secretary telling him the DA was on the line for him. Mike didn't want to hand over their case for several reasons first it's their case! Any detective would fight tooth and nail before they just roll over and let someone get credit for solving the case after they've put in all the hard work on it. Second, he has no idea how they stumbled upon this witness. There could be all sorts of reasons why she could have been out in the woods that time of morning wheeling a huge plastic container, if only he could think of one. Rumors were already beginning to spread about the witness naming Agent Jackson as a suspect in the disappearance of Fred Simmons.

Dodging the question of how they came about Drew Smith in the first place, Mike starts firing off a list of things that needed to be done.

"First, we need to find out if what he said was true. We need to bring in his wife and question her to see if their stories match. He could be the killer for all we know," Mike says desperately. He brought up the fact that Anna would have to be brought in as well to stand in a line-up. He could not believe what he just said but at this point, he would do anything to save Anne. He was also trying to stall for a little more time as Anne was in the hallway pacing back and forth on her cell phone. Losing the argument, Mike headed and went to collect his case files and notes when Anne came back into the squad room.

"Captain wants our files," Mike said to Anne.

Anne takes a deep breath, shakes her head and begins to collect her notes and files.

"Hey Captain asks how we came about the Smiths anyway. I didn't know what to tell him. How did you know about them?" Mike asks, hoping she did not think he was accusing her also. Without saying anything she just handed over her files with the report she got from Linda, a crime tech, that showed the DNA results from the gum she collected in the woods that night on top. As Mike looks at the report, Anne looks at her cell phone and walks away towards the door. Captain Santana waves Mike into his office as he ends his phone call.

"Here are all of our files and notes since we arrived here," Mike said. "Anne found gum near the tire tracks in the woods that came back to Drew Smith," he added.

"Where's Anne?" Captain Santana asks.

In the squad room, everyone's facial expression changed in an instant. As Anne and Anna walked through the department towards the captain's office all eyes were on them. Man, news travels fast Anne thought. She was not sure if they were in shock that she was suspected of being the serial killer or that her sister might be. Anna did not care if people were staring at her, but Anne could not stand it. They make it to the office and was just about to close the door when they hear,

"Hey wait up. Don't start without me!" someone yells from across the room.

Everyone looks up to see a 5'6 brown skinned black woman maneuvering through the desks towards the captain's office as if she's been there a million times before.

Anne hadn't heard that voice in a couple of months now let alone seen the face that goes with that voice in about three years now. With everyone's career keeping them so busy it was impossible to catch up regularly. But just like when they were younger every time Anne, Anna, or their mother Laura, which was often, got into any trouble they would call her. Heck, she's on speed dial on all their phones and they are on hers. It was Tasha Williams, their lawyer and best friend. Heck, she is practically a sister. They immediately met up in the middle of the squad room and hugged which seemed like forever. Tears welled up in Anne's eyes and she could not narrow down as to exactly why. Tasha heard a sniff and responded.

"It's okay. I'm here. I dropped everything when I got the call. You know nothing comes before family. When you're in trouble and you need me, I'm there unless I'm dead or in jail myself," Tasha said trying to subside any fear. From what she has heard so far no one is going to jail not today. She's always had a knack for trying to bring a little humor during a bad situation. Anne knew that she would be there for them in a heartbeat like she has so many times before. Tasha is a successful defense attorney. When she told Anne and Anna what she was going to college for after high school they were not shocked. Tasha has always defended anyone in need. She is a nurturer by heart. It is what she does best, take care of those who cannot take care of themselves. She has gotten into countless fights throughout elementary, middle, and high school sticking up for kids that were bullied, and no kid was ever bullied more than Anne and Anna.

Anne and Anna never asked how she knew to come here because they each thought the other had called her.

"When Mike called me, I had to get here right away. I told him I was surprised that you didn't call me, but I get it. Didn't want to be on record as the lead agent on a case calling in a defense attorney to help the suspect and possibly be seen as leaking key evidence when you just would have been an agent calling in help for her little sister," Tasha said as she smiled and winked at Anna. Tasha was thinking of the arguments Anne and Anna had over who was older. Anna would always say they were the same age, and no one is older, but Anne would always stand her ground as big sister because she came out first.

"I hate to break up this family reunion, but we need to get this over with please," Captain Santana says.

"Well don't worry everything is going to be okay." Tasha says to Anne.

"Captain Santana, I need a moment alone with my clients. Thank you," Tasha says.

The three of them went into an interrogation room to talk.

"So, what is going on?" Tasha asked.

"To make a long story short, while investigating the Fred Simmons case, I found a chewed-up piece of gum. The DNA came back to a man named Drew Smith. Mike and I went to question him and his wife at their home. They stated they were in the park near where we believe Mr. Simmons was kidnapped. While asking questions I got the feeling they knew something, but they claimed they didn't hear or see anything. We decided to go back and question the couple again when Drew Smith came in to talk to us. It was in this interrogation room when he stated they saw me in the woods that night with a dolly carrying a large plastic container," Anne stated.

"Has any charges been brought against either of you?" Tasha asks.

"No." Anne and Anna respond at the same time.

"Well, I'm advising both of you to say nothing. Anne, I want you to contact me when you are to report to Internal Affairs to make a statement," Tasha stated.

Tasha and Anna looked over at Anne with concern.

"Anne, are you alright? You look like you are about to pass out" Anna asks.

"I just need some air," Anne says as she walks out the door.

Anne did not know what to do or where to go. Everything was happening so fast. She felt like she could not breathe. She had to get out of there, so she went out of the squad room and ended up in the stairwell. Standing at the top of the stairs right outside the exit door Anne stared off into space. Tears of frustration started to roll down her cheeks and her fist was clenched so tight her nails may have broken the skin on her palms. At least it felt that way not paying attention to her surroundings because she assumed no one else was around. She turns to go back in to at least watch the interview from the other side of the two-way mirror and Mike was standing there. He has always been there for her so, there was no reason for him to not be here at one of the worst moments of her career, the worst moment of her life. When she turned around to leave, Mike opened his arms and hugged her. She was too upset to ask him what he was doing and accepted the embrace she did not realize she needed because the flood of tears poured down like a broken river dam.

She steps back out of his arms and looks up at him.

"Thanks for being there for me," she says to him as she gets her bearings.

She starts wiping her eyes with her hands but wasn't sure what she was going to do about the snot running down her nose. Leave it to mike to read her mind and he hands her his handkerchief. Not knowing exactly what to say, he responds "no problem anytime,"

"I guess I need to get back in there. I don't want my sister to think that I've abandoned her or worse think that I believe she has anything to do with it," she says, handing him back his handkerchief. He kind of wished she would have kept it.

They walk back into the hall heading to the interrogation room where she left Anna and Tasha. She has always looked out for Anna and was not about to stop now. As they get to the room they did not expect Anna to be answering questions.

"Can you tell me where you were that night?" Captain Santana asks Anna.

Just as Tasha has drilled into her head about being questioned by authorities, only answer questions when your lawyer is present and only if she tells you it's okay to answer. Anna looks over to Tasha and she gives the nod to answer the question.

"In the gym training for my fight coming up," Anna says.

"Did anyone see you there? Can anyone vouch for you?" the captain asks.

Looking over at Tasha, Anna says "I think the gym manager was leaving when I was coming in,"

"Why would the manager leave someone at the gym alone? Shouldn't they be there in case of an emergency?" the captain asks not even giving her a chance to answer the first question.

"Fighters that are assigned to the team use that gym whenever they get ready. Only unsigned fighters that pay to use it must have an appointment and the manager must be on site. They would like for our trainers to be with us but it's not mandatory," Anna tells him.

"Are there any cameras in the gym?" the captain says

"We have a cameraman that records our sparring matches, but I don't know if there are surveillance cameras," Anna says lying knowing that they do.

A couple of days later Tasha, sitting in her office, receives a phone call from the District Attorney. They were formally charging Anna Jackson with kidnapping and murder. She ended the call letting him know that she will be surrendering her client in the morning. She knew all they had was circumstantial evidence.

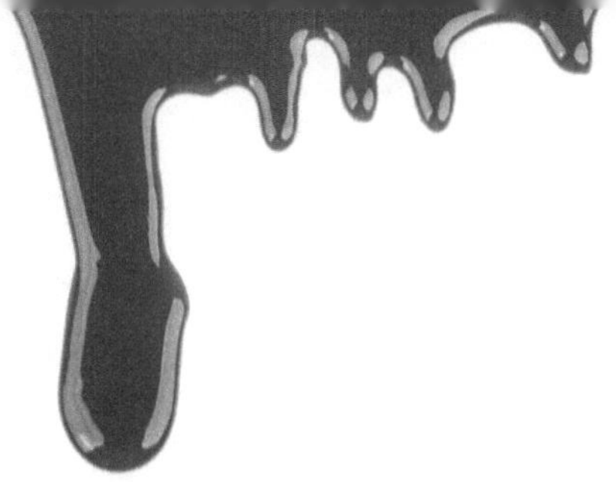

Chapter 17

Sitting in the courtroom listening to the prosecutor tell the world how Anna was responsible for Fred Simmons' death seemed like a dream. The jury was attentive to what he had to say. He brought up the fact that they had two eyewitnesses placing Anna at the scene and DNA evidence found on a small piece of tissue near where the body was found belonging to Anna as well.

"Ladies and gentlemen, please do not look at Ms. Jackson's petite body stature and assume she could not have kidnapped him all by herself. Ms. Jackson is a world UFC champion," he stated pointing to the white board in the middle of the courtroom. It was a video compilation of Anna training and competitions. It seemed they found the most gruesome matches where it looked as if she was actually trying to kill her opponent. It is no secret that she has a temper. Tasha was now giving her opening statement. She ended her statement asking the jury to remember that the prosecution must prove guilt beyond a shadow of a doubt and if not, they must find her client not guilty. For two days the prosecution called expert witnesses to talk about their process and the conclusions they got from the evidence they collected. Drew and Stacy Smith were called to testify as to what they saw. On the third day the prosecution called in their last witness to testify. Laura Jackson, Anna and Annes' mother.

With the shock and awe heard through the courtroom along with the whispers of the people in the seats filled the courtroom. Anne sat inside the courtroom, on one of the benches, with a look of rage on her face. Her mother was giving testimony for the prosecution as it turned out. The prosecutor had investigators dig deep into their family background. They talked to anyone that knew Anna. He did an excellent job painting Anna as a serial killer in the making since early childhood. No one could understand why the prosecution would call the defendant's mother to the stand. What could they have possibly found out that the defense didn't know about? Anne thought.

"Ms. Jackson, could you please tell the court who you are and why you are here testifying for the prosecution today," DA Jones stated.

"I am Anna's mom and I wanted to say that all of this is happening because of me," she stated. As her mother, the only thing she could testify to is her daughter's character growing up and now.

"Can you explain why you believe that you are responsible for your daughter, the defendant, being tried for kidnapping and murder," DA Jones asks.

"I didn't think much of it when the news talked about all those men that were found dead in the Navy. But when my other daughter Anne called me to say that Anna was a suspect, I knew it was my fault. See I uhh…umm I told my girls a lie about something that happened to me a long time ago," Laura stated.

"And what was the lie you told your daughters?" DA Jones asked.

Looking down at her lap Laura said under her breath "I told them I was raped by a guy in the Navy, and he was their father,"

"I'm sorry Laura, could you repeat that so everyone in the courtroom can hear you please," DA Jones replied.

"I told them I was raped by a guy in the Navy, and he was their father," Laura repeated.

Swore to never tell anyone, not even Tasha, their best friend in the whole world. That secrecy was upheld because the look on Tasha's face when Laura said it proves it. But what was worse was the fact that Laura lied about being raped. Anna lost her cool. She jumped up from her seat and yelled "Are you kidding me!"

Anne just sat in her seat motionless. The chatter in the courtroom could be heard down the hallway. The judge banging his gavel yelled "Order! Order! We will recess and be back tomorrow morning at 8am,"

Anna sat in a chair in a small room, used by counsel and their clients to have privacy, waiting on her attorney. When Tasha comes into the room, Anna puts her head down on the table. It never occurred to her to tell Tasha about her mom because it was a secret from so long ago and they never brought it up again since they were little.

Walking into the room everyone was there including her mother. Laura was standing in the corner leaning back against the wall head down fiddling with her fingers like she always did when she was nervous. Her sister sat down with her head down on the table and Tasha sat across from her sister with her elbows on the table and leaning her forehead on her fingertips. When Anne walks in, all eyes lock on her. At that moment she didn't want to be in that room it seems everyone was waiting for her to take charge of what happened next. Not wanting to let her sister and Tasha down she turned to her mom. "So, you're telling me that you lied all these years?!!" she said. Throwing everyone off breaking the silence and directing the question at her mother. To tell the truth she didn't know what to say to her sister and she needed a little more time to gather her thoughts.

"Wait what?" Laura says confusingly. "I thought we were here to talk about Anna's case!" Trying to get the attention off her but it wasn't working. Tears start to stream down her face, and she starts pacing.

"Okay Okay. I'm going to tell you the truth. You got to understand that at the time when you guys were little, I didn't think you would understand if I told you the truth and I didn't want you thinking bad of me," Laura says looking back and forth between the twins possibly looking for any type of reaction.

No response just curious looks staring back at her. Tasha was even confused because she had no clue about this all these years.

"When you got older and started asking about your dad, I didn't know what to say. I panicked. I just didn't want you to think less of me than you already did because of my drinking," Laura continued. She paused in hopes someone would say something. Tasha wanted to say something but felt it wasn't her place to.

Anna screams angrily, "Get to the point!"

Pacing back and forth while pulling her hair back she said "well before you guys were born I...I...would do certain things to support myself. I never went to college okay. I slept with guys for money,"

"You were a prostitute?!" Anna says with a disgustingly confused look on her face.

"See! See that was the reaction I didn't want to face!" Laura cries.

"So, you made up a story about being raped and that we were the product of it. You didn't think that would be worse than telling us the truth?" Anna says.

"I didn't have a great relationship with my mom. She didn't have one with hers and it was just awful growing up hating her and not having her around. And I didn't want you guys to hate me. I wanted us to be close, you know. I didn't have a story planned out about your dad and when you asked me I panicked and that was the first thing that came to mind." Laura says.

"So, what is the truth? Is grandma dead or alive? Do you know who our father is or not?" Anne says in a soft tone that broke the silence in the room.

Laura looks at Anne with desperation like she knows that at least one of them was going to be upset but she never thought that they would both turn against her. For a couple of minutes, everyone just stared at Laura with anticipation waiting for answers to all the questions that were thrown at her. About two hours had gone by but it seemed like just minutes when Anna broke the silence.

"I want to plead guilty," Anna says.

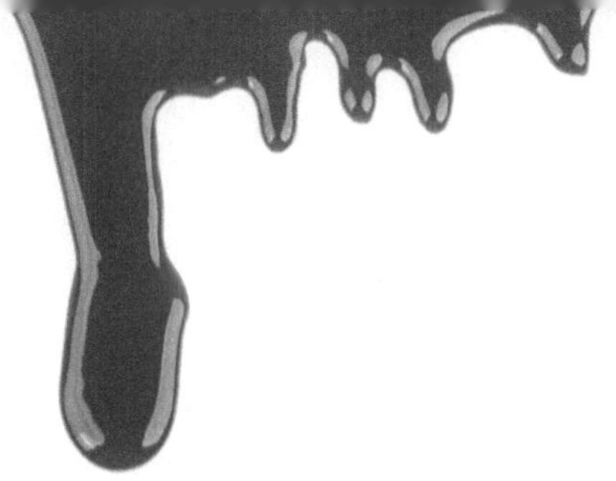

Chapter 18

ANNE STUDIES THE LOOK ON her sister's face, and it breaks her heart, but it is not the look of someone finally caught after committing horrible crimes. Never in a million years would she have thought that it would be centered on her family. Family secrets have unraveled in the past few weeks that have hit her like a ton of bricks. Her mother confessing to not being raped but being a prostitute and all of the stories about the horrific ordeal she fed them caused her to decide to dedicate her life to hunting down bad guys and bringing them to justice. Anna became a UFC fighter only by chance because she trained only to protect herself from men like that. The paths they chose in life were all based on a lie from the one person that meant the world to them. She didn't know which emotion should take over right now sister, daughter, or detective. It took her a while to realize the need to get justice for her mom was the driving force to become a cop. All of this made no sense to her. She had no clue about what to do with all of this information. All she did know for sure was that nothing will ever be the same after this. Nothing.

Tasha walked out of the room after hearing the entire story and shedding a few tears with her best friends to find the prosecutor.

"Can I talk to you for a second?" Tasha says as she stands in front of the prosecutor who was too busy with whatever was on his phone to notice that she was even coming his way.

"What's up?" He responds.

"As much as I hate to say this, my client wants to talk about a plea deal," she says, sounding as if one would not want to admit it.

There was enough evidence to prosecute, and the defendant's mother just provided motive, something that was not present at the beginning of the trial. A federal agent's twin sister has been arrested for the crimes. Everyone was saying that the reason why it took so long to catch her was that her sister was covering for her or was in on it with her.

"Let's talk," he says.

Chapter 19

ANNA DIDN'T WANT TO SEE anyone. She declined visitors. She even declined to see Tasha, her counsel, best friend and sister since childhood. All communications came from another associate who works with Tasha. The judge was going to give her the death penalty but after reviewing the circumstances of the case he decided on life without the possibility of parole. Everyone wanted to wrap this case up. The public wanted someone to pay.

Anne has taken time off work, not voluntarily, to get herself together and to make sure her sister is okay. She is concerned that Anna has closed herself off in a shell. After it first happened the media had a field day. Every news station, the front page of every newspaper, Twitter, Facebook, Instagram, and any other media outlet ran the story of the serial killing UFC champ 24/7. The only visitors that are allowed up to her condo are Mike, who has been by her side throughout this whole thing, and Tasha. So, the knock at the door did not surprise her but seeing two men dressed in suits on the other side of the door did. She is not sure what they could be here for.

"Anne Jackson?" one of the men asks.

"Yes," she answered with a confused look on her face.

"Sorry to bother you but I'm Detective Samuels and this is my partner Detective Matthews," he says.

Maybe a perp she put away is claiming they are innocent and that she set them up or something. That, she could deal with and now praying this has nothing to do with her sister.

"I'm sorry to inform you that your sister was found dead this morning in her cell," Det. Samuels says unapologetically.

"What?" Anne asks in shock.

"She hung herself last night. She left several notes, and one was addressed to you," Samuels says, cutting Jones off thinking he could have been a little more empathetic towards a fellow detective.

They handed her the note, told her again how sorry they were for her loss and turned to leave. She closed the door and just stood there staring at the note. Not able to move her legs. She was stuck in another world when the phone rang. All she knew was that whatever happens from this point it can't get any worse.

"Hello," she says, trying to keep her composure.

"Hey," says Mike, a comforting voice on the other end which is needed at this moment. Before she can tell him about her sister, he hits her with some bad news of his own and at that moment she wasn't sure which was worse.

"Another body was found."

www.ingramcontent.com/pod-product-compliance
Lightning Source LLC
Chambersburg PA
CBHW020050310726
48970CB00007B/2502